THE HOUSE ON DIRTY-THIRD STREET

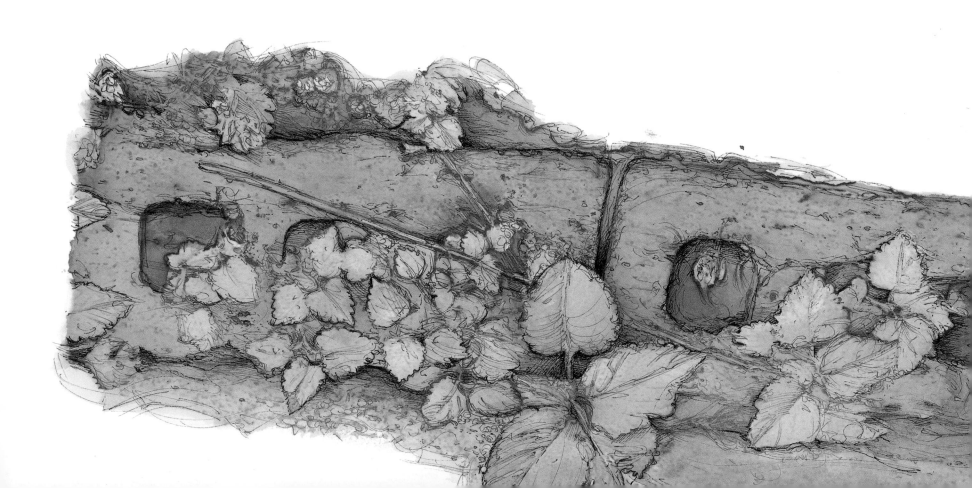

For Ken and Michelle Blackwood and
everyone who lends a hand to help people
improve their lives

—J. S. K.

To my wife Noni and daughter Nina,
the two people I love and admire the most,
and to the "Fernández Family House" for
your awesome help

—T. G.

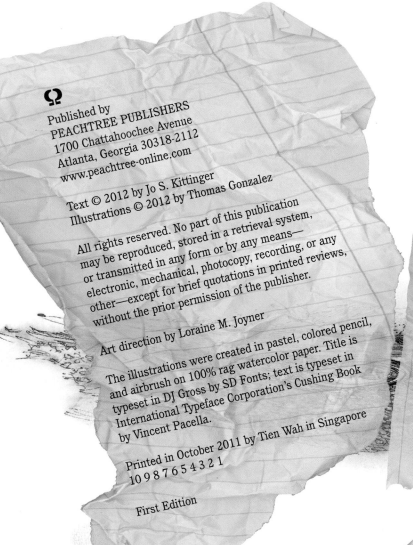

Published by
PEACHTREE PUBLISHERS
1700 Chattahoochee Avenue
Atlanta, Georgia 30318-2112
www.peachtree-online.com

Text © 2012 by Jo S. Kittinger
Illustrations © 2012 by Thomas Gonzalez

Art direction by Loraine M. Joyner

The illustrations were created in pastel, colored pencil,
and airbrush on 100% rag watercolor paper. Title is
typeset in DJ Gross by SD Fonts; text is typeset in
International Typeface Corporation's Cushing Book
by Vincent Pacella.

Printed in October 2011 by Tien Wah in Singapore
10 9 8 7 6 5 4 3 2 1

First Edition

Library of Congress Cataloging-in-Publication Data

Kittinger, Jo S.
The house on Dirty-Third Street / written by Jo S. Kittinger ; illustrated by Thomas Gonzalez.
    p. cm.
Summary: A mother and daughter work to turn a hopeless, rundown, and dirty old house into
a loving family home with hard work, faith, and the support of their new friends and neighbors.
ISBN 978-1-56145-619-2 / 1-56145-619-5
[1. Buildings--Repair and reconstruction--Fiction. 2. Home--Fiction. 3. Neighborhoods--
Fiction. 4. Neighbors--Fiction. 5. Faith--Fiction.] I. Gonzalez, Thomas, 1959- ill. II. Title.
PZ7.K67152Ho 2012
[E]--dc23

2011020458

THE HOUSE ON DIRTY-THIRD STREET

Jo S. Kittinger

illustrated by
Thomas Gonzalez

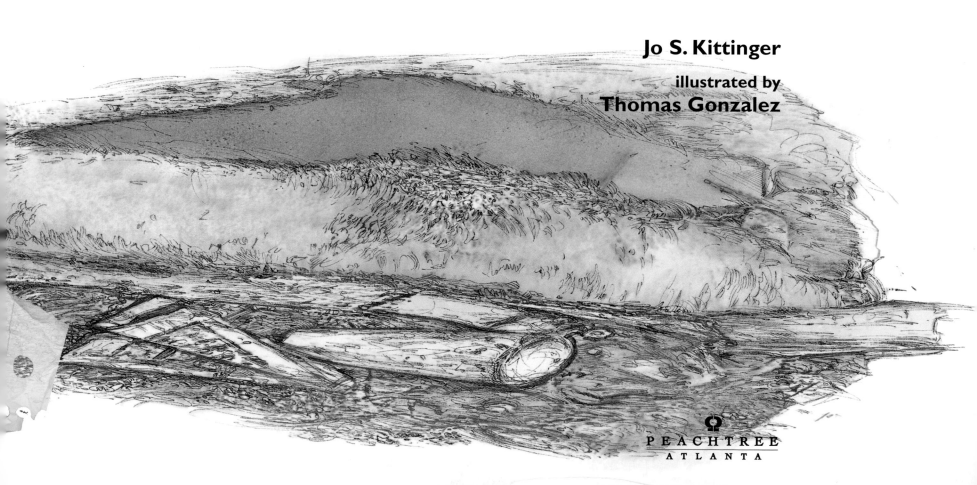

PEACHTREE
ATLANTA

Mom said starting over would be an adventure,
so I imagined a tropical island with palm trees and
buried treasure.

Not this.

All the houses on Thirty-third Street
were old and run down, but the one with
the For Sale sign was the worst. I'd call the
whole place "*Dirty*-third Street."
"It's perfect," said Mom.
"It doesn't look perfect to me," I said.
"It's perfect," she said, "because we can afford it."

"Try looking at it through eyes of faith," said Mom.
I squinted and tilted my head. "It still looks horrible to me."

Soon the house on Dirty-third Street was
ours. But before we could start moving things
in, we had to move trash out.

A neighbor watched from her front yard. "Hi there," Mom called out to her. "I've hired a man to take a load to the dump. Is there anything you'd like to add to our trash pile?"

"I don't know..." The woman sounded like she hadn't trusted anyone in years.

Before long, Mom and I were wrestling
an old sofa from Mrs. Huddle's porch
to the curb.

By the end of the day, word had spread.
The pile in front of our house became a mountain.

The bathroom was so filthy it made shivers run down my back. "It will look and smell better when it's clean," Mom told me. So, all day Saturday we swept and scrubbed. I was dog-tired and grouchy.

Clearing away the trash and dirt just made it obvious how ugly the place truly was. "This house will never look good," I mumbled.

"You may be right," said Mom. She sank to the floor in the corner. "What was I thinking?"

I slumped down beside her and leaned my head against her shoulder. "Remind me," I said. "How did you see it?"

"I saw a pretty white house with blue shutters," she said. "There were flowers on the porch. The windows sparkled and curtains danced in the breeze. The kitchen was full of friends and I smelled cookies hot from the oven."

Mom's eyes got dreamy looking. Then she shook her head. "I miss our old neighborhood," she said, "and my friends from church."

"We can make new friends." I stood up and dusted myself off. "I saw a church a few blocks away. Let's go in the morning."

After breakfast we walked to the church. In Sunday school, the teacher asked if anyone had prayer requests. "We just moved here and our house needs lots of work," I said. "I don't want Mom to cry any more. Please pray that she can still see the house with eyes of faith, and that I, somehow, can see it that way too."

Not long after we got home, I heard a knock at the door.

"Good afternoon, ma'am," a man said when Mom opened the door.

"At church this morning I heard you could use some help around here."

Mom was showing him the broken bricks on the porch when

Mrs. Huddle walked across the street. "Thought these might cheer

things up," she said. "Once upon a time, my flowers used to bloom on

near about every porch in this neighborhood."

Mrs. Huddle started
transplanting the flowers into
an old cement planter in the yard.
A few minutes later, a car pulled up.

Next thing I knew, a whole family was heading our
way, including my Sunday School teacher and a girl my age.

"Welcome to the neighborhood," my teacher said.
"My husband's a great handyman."

The man took one look at the peeling paint and
then pulled out a cell phone. "Let me get a few more
folks over here," he said.

By the next weekend, our house looked
like an anthill. Men on the roof hammered
shingles. My new friends and I scraped peeling
paint. A lady fixed loose bricks on the porch.
Another neighbor worked
on the plumbing.

The sun settled behind our house and the workers took a break. I opened the door and the smell of cookies, hot from the oven, made my mouth water. Finally I could see it—our place, as Mom had—through eyes of faith. We had found our perfect home.

And somehow I knew that I wouldn't
call it Dirty-third Street anymore.